Cinderella

The Great Mouse Mistake

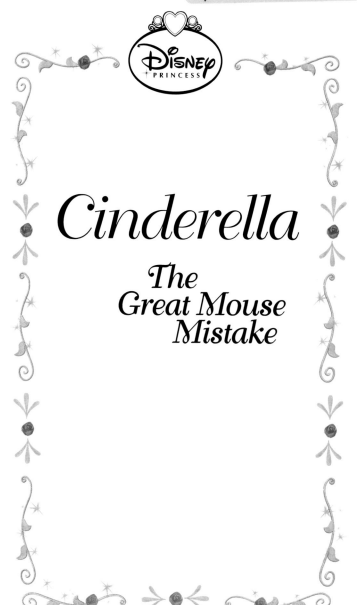

This edition published by Parragon in 2012
Parragon
Queen Street House
4 Queen Street
Bath BA1 1HE, UK
www.parragon.com

ISBN 978-1-4454-9665-8
Printed in China

Cinderella

The Great Mouse Mistake

By Ellie O'Ryan
Illustrated by Studio IBOIX
and the Disney Storybook Artists

Bath • New York • Singapore • Hong Kong • Cologne • Delhi
Melbourne • Amsterdam • Johannesburg • Shenzhen

Chapter One

"A trap?" Cinderella cried. "Why didn't you say so?"

In an instant, Cinderella ran out of her tiny bedroom, down the steep attic stairs and through the long hallway of the fancy château in which she lived. A brown mouse, wearing an orange jacket and a pointy red hat, followed behind her as fast as his little paws could carry him. It wasn't every day that a new mouse got caught in a trap, but when it happened, Cinderella was always there and ready to help!

And that was just one of the reasons why all the little mice who lived in the big château loved her. Cinderella's kind heart and warm smile made everyone happy!

Everyone, that is, but Lady Tremaine, Cinderella's cruel stepmother, and Lady Tremaine's horrible daughters, Drizella and Anastasia. Lady Tremaine and her daughters were very mean to Cinderella. They made her live in a cramped, drafty room in the attic. She had to do all the chores. And she had to wait on them hand and foot!

But even though her stepmother and stepsisters were not nice to her, it was in

Cinderella's nature to treat everyone kindly. Especially anyone who needed her help, like the small mouse who was crying in the trap at the end of the hall.

"Poor little thing," Cinderella said in a gentle voice. She opened the trap so that the mouse could come out. He was shaking and very scared.

"Don't worry," said Jaq, the mouse standing next to Cinderella. He smiled at the nervous little mouse. "She is our friend!"

Cinderella looked at the mouse in the cage, who was still shaking. She placed her hand at the opening of the trap to help the mouse get out. She looked at him closely. "We have to give you a name," she said. "How about Octavius? Gus for short!"

Cinderella reached for a set of tiny mouse clothes that she had in her pocket. She pulled a yellow shirt over Gus's round tummy. Then she put a pointy green cap on his head. He looks perfect, Cinderella thought happily.

Gus smiled shyly. He was feeling better already!

"Now I've got to get to work," Cinderella said. "See that Gus keeps out of trouble, Jaq. And don't forget to warn him about that pesky old cat!"

Humming a pretty song, Cinderella hurried off towards the kitchen. She had a lot of chores to do. She had to feed the chickens; Bruno, the big old hound dog; and Lucifer, the mean old cat. And of course, she had to serve breakfast to Lady Tremaine, Drizella

and Anastasia. They would not be happy if she was late!

Jaq grabbed Gus's paw and led him downstairs. "Lotsa mice live here," he told Gus. "Suzy, Perla, Mert, Bert, Luke – wait until you meet them. We have lots of fun together. They'll be your new friends!"

Gus looked over at Jaq. A big grin spread across his face.

"And Cinderella is a friend to all the mice," Jaq continued. "And the birds, and the dog and even . . . the mean cat. Cinderella makes us clothes and gives us food! Like – breakfast!"

Jaq and Gus scurried along the kitchen wall to the courtyard, where Cinderella was busy feeding the chickens. Then Cinderella noticed Jaq and Gus standing in the doorway. "Here you go, you two," she said cheerfully. Then she tossed them a large handful of corn.

Gus looked at all of the corn that was on the ground in front of him. He scurried about, picking up as much as he could carry. Soon he was holding a stack of corn that was almost as tall as he was!

"Hurry up!" called Jaq. His little pockets were overflowing with corn. "Lucifer is coming!"

"Lucifer?" repeated Gus. He looked very confused.

"The cat!" Jaq cried. He grabbed Gus by the arm and ran towards the mouse hole in the wall.

All of sudden, Gus understood why Jaq was in such a hurry. A big, black cat slowly walked into the courtyard. He was licking his lips and flicking his tail.

Cinderella's clear voice rang out across the courtyard. "Lucifer! Don't bother those mice or you won't get any cream for breakfast," she warned the cat. Lucifer eyed the mice for a moment and then crept away.

Jaq and Gus made it to the mouse hole and squeezed themselves inside. That was close! Gus thought.

"Cinderella is so nice," Jaq said with a big grin. "She always takes such very good care of us!"

"I really like Cinderelly!" Gus agreed. He'd only known her for a little while, and already she had saved him from a trap, given him some clothes, served him breakfast and protected him from Lucifer. She was the nicest lady he had ever met!

Suddenly Gus had a great idea. He wanted to do something for Cinderella to show her how thankful he was. Something nice. Something special. Something big!

"Let's go," Jaq said. He patted his pockets, which were full of corn. "All the other mice are going to want breakfast – and we can bring it to them!"

Gus quickly nibbled a few pieces of corn, then handed the rest to Jaq. "You go," he said. "I am going to surprise Cinderelly with a present!"

"Okay, but make sure you watch out

for Lucifer!" Jaq told Gus.

"Okay!" Gus replied. Then he peeked out of the mouse hole and looked both ways. There was no sign of the big, mean cat. He scurried back out into the courtyard. Gus had the whole yard to himself to think up the perfect surprise for Cinderella!

But what would that be? Gus's tiny face scrunched up as he tried to think of a great idea. He could make Cinderella something to wear, like a pretty scarf. But he didn't know how to sew. What about a beautiful painting? But he wasn't an artist.

Suddenly, Gus smelled something very delightful! What could it be? He put his nose in the air and sniffed again.

Then he noticed a beautiful rosebush. It

was covered with enormous pink roses. Gus knew that he'd found it – the perfect present for Cinderella!

He scurried across the courtyard as fast as he could. He climbed up the rosebush and quickly began to gnaw on each branch,

carefully avoiding the thorns. Gus filled his arms with the pretty roses. It would take several trips to carry all the flowers up to Cinderella's room in the attic – and he couldn't wait to get started! I hope she likes them, he thought happily.

Chapter Two

*F*or the rest of the morning, Gus was very nervous. When would Cinderella go up to the attic and find the surprise? But Gus soon realized that she was much too busy to go to the attic during the day. She had to scrub the floors, sweep the halls, wash the clothes, clean the kitchen, do the mending – and, of course, cater to her stepmother and stepsisters. Phew! Gus was tired just thinking about it!

Oh, well, Gus thought. Cinderelly's gotta go to sleep at night. Then she'll find the flowers and have sweet dreams! He closed his eyes as he imagined how surprised she would be when she found the roses. He really hoped that she would love them!

But Gus's daydream was interrupted by a loud shriek. "My roses! My beautiful, prize-winning roses! Gone!" he heard a woman suddenly scream.

Gus's eyes grew wide. Uh-oh, he thought. That doesn't sound very good!

The entire household rushed to the garden, including Gus. Cinderella was the first to arrive. There, she found Lady Tremaine staring at the bare rosebush. Her mouth had dropped open in shock.

"Oh, no!" gasped Cinderella. "The pink pearl roses! Who would have done such a thing?"

"I don't know who would have done something like this," Lady Tremaine replied coldly. "But I intend to find out. Look!" she suddenly exclaimed, pointing to the ground. "Some pink petals from my beautiful rosebush. It appears we have a clumsy thief on our hands! And I'm going to get to the bottom of this right now!"

"Yeah!" sneered Anastasia. "Clumsy *and* foolish!" She laughed gleefully.

"Are you saying that you stole the roses?" Drizella asked her sister nastily. "Because you're the clumsiest fool I know!" She gave Anastasia a mean look.

"Girls! Girls!" ordered Lady Tremaine. "That is *not* going to help us find the thief." Then Lady Tremaine looked at

Cinderella suspiciously.

"Me? But how can you – " Cinderella began. "I would never – "

"Follow the petals!" Lady Tremaine shouted angrily. "They will lead us to whoever is responsible for this!"

Everyone quickly walked across the garden. The trail of rose petals led them through the garden, across the courtyard, into the château, and up the creaky, winding staircase that led to the attic.

Gus's heart started to pound wildly. They would find the roses in Cinderella's room – and think that she had taken them! He didn't want her to get in trouble.

"This doesn't make any sense!" Cinderella exclaimed as she followed Lady Tremaine up the attic stairs. "I didn't cut the roses! I've been busy doing chores all day!"

But Lady Tremaine didn't even bother to answer her. With a loud slam, she flung open the door to Cinderella's bedroom. It was filled with Lady Tremaine's roses!

"Then how do you explain this?" Cinderella's stepmother asked her.

Tears filled Cinderella's eyes. "But I didn't steal the roses!" she cried. "I would never do that. You must believe me!"

"Oh, so I suppose someone else cut down my precious blooms and decided to hide them in your bedroom?" Lady Tremaine snapped.

"But Stepmother – " Cinderella began.

"Silence!" Lady Tremaine barked. "Not another word from you until you are ready

to apologize. And until then, I'll just have to find more chores for you to do."

"Wait! Stepmother, I didn't – " Cinderella started.

But with a swish of her silk gown, Lady Tremaine swept out of the attic. Anastasia and Drizella quickly followed behind her.

Cinderella sat down on her bed and started to cry. "I would never steal Stepmother's roses! Why won't she believe me?" she said aloud.

From the doorway, Gus gulped nervously. He crept across the room to Cinderella, then climbed up the wooden bedpost and sat next to her on the bed. "There, there, Cinderelly," he said, patting her shoulder. "Don't cry. Everything will be okay."

Cinderella looked down at Gus and smiled. "Thank you, Gus. What a kind mouse you are," she said. But then she noticed how worried he looked.

"What's wrong, Gus?" she asked. "Do you know who stole the roses and then put them in my room?"

Gus nodded miserably. "It was – it was – it was me," he stuttered.

"You?" Cinderella asked. "Oh, Gus, why did you do such a thing?"

"Because I wanted to do something nice for you!" Gus exclaimed. "I didn't know the roses belonged to anybody."

"It was very sweet of you to want to do something nice for me, Gus," Cinderella told him. She looked at him kindly.

Gus beamed up at Cinderella. He was so glad that she wasn't mad at him!

"But we must always be careful not to take something that belongs to someone else," Cinderella continued. "Those roses were very special to Stepmother. In fact, every June she enters them into the village gardening competition. She'll be so very disappointed when she can't enter the contest this year. We have to do something."

Gus looked down sadly. He never wanted to cause such trouble.

Cinderella stared into the distance. Suddenly, her eyes lit up. "I know! We'll go to the village and buy a new rosebush for Stepmother as a surprise!" Cinderella exclaimed. "She'll be so happy to have her special roses growing in the garden again!"

Gus's eyes grew wide. "Village? What's that, Cinderelly?" he asked.

"Oh, Gus! The village is a wonderful place!" Cinderella exclaimed. "There are rows of shops and houses right next to one another. The streets are full of carts and carriages and people and horses!" Cinderella took one look at Gus's excited face and smiled.

Cinderella thought for a moment. "I know," she said. "Since you've never been to a village before, you'll have to come with me and help me pick out a new rosebush," she told Gus.

"Okay!" Gus said excitedly. He had just learned what a village was, and already he couldn't wait to go!

Cinderella hurried over to the table and picked up a small basket. She lined it with a pretty silk pillow and a soft handkerchief.

"Here, Gus, hop in the basket," she told him. "We should leave right away. The sooner we get back, the sooner we can surprise Stepmother with a beautiful new rosebush!"

Chapter Three

*T*he warm sun shone down on Cinderella and Gus as they walked along the road to the village. It was a beautiful day.

"Luckily, I ran out of silver polish just the other day," Cinderella was telling Gus. "That's why Lady Tremaine is letting me go to the village before my chores are finished."

But as Cinderella chatted, Gus could

hardly pay any attention. He was too excited. What would the village look like? What kinds of things would he see? And most importantly, would there be yummy foods to eat there? He sure hoped so. Even though he had had breakfast earlier, he was starving again!

Fortunately, Gus didn't have to wait long to find out. Soon the buildings of the village appeared. Gus poked his head out of the basket as he tried to get a better view.

Everything looked amazing! Gus hadn't expected to see colourful banners fluttering in the breeze. He also was surprised by the jolly sounds of trumpets and drums. The little mouse smiled. This was even better than he had imagined!

"Look, Gus!" Cinderella exclaimed. "I forgot that the annual village fair is today. Oh, it's so much fun! There are games and music and a big parade and lots of delicious food. Even the Prince and the rest of the royal family come to the fair. Oh, it's just absolutely wonderful!"

Then Cinderella paused. "Gus, the village can be a very busy place," she warned him. "Especially when the fair comes to town. So I think it might be best if you stay tucked in the basket, all right? You can still see everything that happens – just peek out the slats of the basket."

"Okay," Gus promised, nodding his head eagerly. He didn't want to cause any more trouble for Cinderella.

"First stop, Madame Gilmore's flower shop!" Cinderella announced. She walked over to a small building that was covered in dark green vines. When she opened the door, a little bell rang.

Inside, the shop was quiet and dim and filled with all sorts of beautiful plants and flowers. Gus peeked his head out of the basket and cautiously looked around. "Cinderelly!" he squeaked. "These flowers are beautiful!" Gus took a deep breath as he smelled all the wonderful fragrances from the blooms.

"I know!" Cinderella cried. "Isn't it lovely?"

Just then, a woman walked in carrying a large bouquet of daffodils. "Ah! Welcome,"

she said, wiping dirt off her hands as she
greeted Cinderella. Gus quickly dove back
into the basket.

"Hello, Madame Gilmore," Cinderella
said. "How are you today?"

"Very well indeed, especially now that you've come to my shop," Madame Gilmore replied. "Are you looking for something special today? Perhaps an orange tree for the orchard? A flowering shrub for a hedge? Or how about some plants or flowerpots for the terrace?"

"I would like to buy a pink pearl rose-bush, please," Cinderella replied politely.

"But of course," Madame Gilmore said. "I just received a pink pearl rosebush last week. Look how magnificent it is!" she exclaimed, pointing to it.

"It's perfect!" cried Cinderella. "Stepmother will be absolutely delighted!" Cinderella smiled happily.

"Ah, yes," agreed Madame Gilmore. "This

is her favourite flower, correct?"

"It is," Cinderella responded. "And I need it right away. Could you please deliver it to the château this afternoon?"

"Of course," Madame Gilmore said. "It will be my pleasure."

Cinderella reached into the basket for a gold coin to pay for the rosebush. Gus found one and handed it to her. Madame Gilmore never suspected that the little mouse was in the basket!

"Thank you so much," Cinderella said as she handed over the coin.

"Thank you, my dear," Madame Gilmore answered. "I will deliver the rosebush this afternoon."

With a little wave good-bye, Cinderella

turned and left the flower shop. The village streets seemed to be even noisier and more crowded than when they had arrived. Everyone was thrilled about the fair!

Cinderella opened the lid of the basket and peeked in at Gus. "How are you doing in there, little Gus?" she asked.

"Very good, Cinderelly," the mouse said. "I love the village!"

"So do I," Cinderella said. "But I really should hurry home and get back to my chores. Although the village fair does only come once a year . . . I suppose it wouldn't do any harm to walk around for a little while. There are so many lovely things to see. Would you like that?"

"Oh, yes!" Gus exclaimed.

"Okay!" Cinderella laughed. Then she turned serious. "Now remember, Gus, stay in your basket and keep out of sight when there are people around. We've had quite enough trouble for one day, I think!"

Gus jumped up and gave Cinderella a kiss on the cheek. Then he ducked back into the basket. He peeked through a crack so he could see what was happening.

And what a lot there was to see! There were giant floats for the parade, and stands selling beautiful jewellery, fresh flowers and brightly coloured dresses.

But Gus wasn't interested in the fancy fabrics or sparkly jewels. He was interested in something else – something that made his nose twitch happily.

Gus smelled his favourite food: cake! The sweet scent of vanilla and sugar drifted by in the breeze. His mouth started to water. What he wouldn't do for just a bite – one little delicious bite!

Forgetting his promise to Cinderella, Gus poked his head out of the basket. And then he spotted it: the biggest cake he had ever seen! Across the street, the town baker was proudly putting the finishing touches on a twelve-layer vanilla cake. It was covered with beautiful flowers made out of icing. The King had specifically requested that he make it for the royal family. The baker was very pleased with the way it had turned out. He had worked very hard on it.

Gus couldn't resist. He had to have

at least a tiny nibble of the tasty-looking dessert. He leaped out of the basket and landed on the cobblestoned street. Cinderella was so busy admiring a pretty blue dress that she didn't even notice Gus had left.

The mouse raced across the street and climbed up a rack filled with plates and cups. Gus didn't realize how shaky the rack was as he climbed up it. All he could think about was tasting that cake!

Back across the street, Cinderella sighed happily. "A dress made of pale blue satin would be so elegant," she said to herself. "Maybe someday I'll get to wear a gown like this. After all, one can always dream. Right, Gus?"

But there was no answer.

"Gus?" Cinderella asked again. With a little frown, she peeked into the basket – and realized that Gus was gone!

"Oh, dear!" Cinderella cried. Her voice was filled with worry. "Where did he go?" She bent down to look for Gus under the long tables.

Then Cinderella heard someone scream. "Look out!" they cried. Cinderella stood up and quickly spun around.

The rack of dishes was wobbling back and forth, and everything was about to fall! At the very top stood Gus. He was absolutely terrified.

Cinderella raced across the street. "Jump down, Gus," she whispered, looking around nervously. "Don't worry, I'll catch you!"

Gus squeezed his eyes shut and jumped off the top of the rack.

Thump! He landed safely on the soft pillow Cinderella had put in the basket.

"Are you okay?" Cinderella asked him.

Gus nodded. But before he could say anything, a man suddenly yelled, "The rack is going to fall! Everyone get out of the way! Hurry!"

Cinderella jumped back just in time. The rack crashed to the ground, sending dishes everywhere. The ones that didn't break on the street landed right on the beautiful layer cake, smashing it instantly. It was clear that the lovely cake was ruined.

Gus peeked out the side of the basket at

the broken dishes and the flattened cake. He knew that he'd now caused a much, much bigger problem than taking Lady Tremaine's roses.

Oh, no, Gus thought. What did I do now? It seems all I've been doing today is making more and more trouble!

Chapter Four

The baker couldn't believe what had just happened. "My cake!" he howled. "My masterpiece creation! Twelve layers of sweet, fluffy cake, made with the finest vanilla and sugar in the land! All my hours of preparation. And now it's ruined!"

Gus peeked his face out of the basket sadly. He felt horrible about what had just happened.

Cinderella took a step toward the baker and put her hand on his shoulder. "It was a beautiful cake," she said kindly. "Everyone who saw it knows how hard you worked on it."

"What good is that?" the baker cried. "Now there will be no dessert for the fair! The royal family specifically requested that I bake them the Prince's favourite cake! What am I going to do now?"

"We'll work something out. I promise," Cinderella told him.

"But how?" he asked. "There is not enough time to bake another twelve-layer cake now! The special dessert is always served after the parade. That's in only six hours. I'm doomed!"

Cinderella smiled. "I'll find a way to do it," she said. "Come to Lady Tremaine's château tonight at five o'clock. We'll have a dessert ready for the fair. I promise!"

"A cake," the baker corrected Cinderella.

"It must be a cake!"

Cinderella nodded. "I will make sure of it," she told him.

"Thank you," the baker said, his voice full of relief. "I will pick up the cake at precisely five o'clock this evening." He gave Cinderella a grateful smile.

But as Cinderella turned away to begin the walk home with Gus safely tucked into the basket, her smile quickly faded. How would she ever bake a cake to serve the entire village and the royal family – and get all of her chores done, too?

Cinderella grew more and more worried as she headed to the château. "Oh, Gus, what am I going to do?" she asked. "I've never made a giant cake before! Only regular-size cakes. I just don't know how this is going to be possible." Cinderella looked down and let out a sigh.

Gus pushed back the lid of the basket and climbed out. He was so embarrassed about what had happened.

Then, his eyes suddenly lit up. He tugged at Cinderella's sleeve eagerly. "Cinderelly! Cinderelly! That's it! You figured it out!" he shouted happily.

"What do you mean, Gus?" Cinderella asked.

"Little cakes!" Gus exclaimed. "Making a great, big, giant cake would take too long. But we can make lotsa little cakes – one for everybody!"

"Hmm," Cinderella replied thoughtfully.

"It's a good idea, Gus. But still, making hundreds of cakes will take a lot of time and effort – and I'm just one person."

"One person with a lot of friends," Gus corrected her. "Everybody will help! Jaq and the other mice . . . and the birds . . . and I bet Bruno the dog would help, too!"

Cinderella smiled. "You know, Gus, you might be right. Maybe we can pull this off, after all!"

In a few minutes, Cinderella and Gus arrived back at the château. Luckily, Lady Tremaine had been very busy supervising Anastasia and Drizella's music lesson and hadn't realized that Cinderella had been gone so long.

Meanwhile, Gus raced through the

château to round up all the mice. "Cinderelly needs us," he told them. "Come down to the kitchen right away! Shh! We have to be really, really quiet!"

A few moments later, Gus found Bruno asleep in the kitchen. Gus woke him up. "Bruno, we need your help," the mouse pleaded. "Will you join us, please?"

Bruno slowly got up off the floor and yawned. He wagged his tail and gave Gus a small nod.

Then Gus noticed some bluebirds sitting on the windowsill. "Come on!" he exclaimed. "Let's all help Cinderelly!" The birds tweeted happily and followed Gus.

When Cinderella got to the kitchen, she could hardly believe her eyes. A group of mice and birds was gathered and ready to help out. Even Bruno was there, waiting to pitch in.

"Oh, thank you, everyone!" she exclaimed. "Thank you so much! I just know we can get this done with everyone helping. This is going to turn out great!"

"Um, Cinderella?" asked Jaq. "What is going to turn out great? What do you want us to do?"

"We are going to bake cakes!" Cinderella told them. "Hundreds of tiny cakes for the village fair." She quickly explained what had happened earlier that day.

"So now everybody's going to eat our cakes," Gus finished. "Even the Prince and his family!"

"What do you think, everyone?" Cinderella asked hopefully. "Would you be willing to spend the day baking with me? I think it could be a lot of fun."

"Of course we'll help our Cinderelly," Perla said immediately.

Suzy jumped up and clapped her hands. "We can do it! I know we can!" she cried.

"Can we eat some of the cake, too, Cinderella?" Jaq asked shyly.

Cinderella laughed. "Let's focus on the baking first," she said, smiling. "Okay, everybody! Let's start making cakes!"

Chapter Five

"Now, let's see," Cinderella said as she read her favourite cake recipe. "We need flour, sugar, vanilla and butter – good, we've got all that! And eggs and milk . . ." She paused. "Well, I can go out to the barn and milk the cow so that we'll have fresh milk for the cakes. But I need someone to go out to the henhouse and collect the eggs. Are there any volunteers?"

"Let's all go," Gus suggested. "We need lotsa paws to carry lotsa eggs!"

"Good idea," Cinderella agreed. Then she picked up a large wooden milking pail and headed out to the barn. "I'll be back soon!" she called over her shoulder. "Thanks, everybody!"

Gus and Jaq hopped off the table to rush out to the henhouse. But before they even reached the door, Mert grabbed hold of their tails.

"Hold it right there," he squeaked. "How are we going to carry all of the eggs when they're almost as big as we are?"

"Mert's right," Perla said. "We need a plan!"

"All we need to do is think of the fastest and

easiest way to get the eggs from the henhouse to the kitchen," Bert said practically. "That shouldn't be too hard!"

There was silence in the kitchen as each mouse tried to come up with a plan.

"Maybe we could run back and forth carrying an egg each trip," Perla finally suggested.

Luke shook his head. "Too dangerous. What if Lucifer saw us and pounced?"

"We could roll the eggs across the courtyard," Jaq said.

"I don't think that will work," Luke said. "What if as we rolled them they cracked?"

The mice looked at each other nervously. And Bruno didn't have any ideas. He'd fallen asleep under the kitchen table!

It suddenly seemed like getting the eggs from the henhouse to the kitchen was going to be very hard for the little mice.

Gus stared out the window at the henhouse. There just had to be a way to do it. Then he noticed the clothesline that was strung between the henhouse and the kitchen. Suddenly Gus had a great idea!

"The clothesline!" Gus cried. "We can put the eggs in the pockets of the clothes, then pull on the clothesline so that the eggs travel across the courtyard – right to the kitchen!"

"What a good idea!" Suzy exclaimed. She ran over to Gus and gave him a big hug – making him blush bright red!

The mice put Gus's plan into action right away. They ran through the henhouse,

gathering the large eggs. Soon they had collected all the eggs they needed. Jaq grabbed a ladder, and the mice worked on carefully tucking the eggs into the pockets of the clothes hanging on the line.

"Okay, everybody," Gus said. "The eggs are ready to go to the kitchen. We have to be very, very careful that they don't fall – or we won't have enough eggs for the cake!"

The other mice nodded. They did not want to let Cinderella down!

"Jaq, Luke and I will go to the kitchen and pull the clothesline," Gus continued. "Mert will toss the eggs to Perla, who will put them in a basket. Suzy and Bert will push the other end of the clothesline. Everybody ready? Let's go!"

Chapter Six

The mice couldn't wait to put the rest of
their plan into action. They rushed off
to their places, and slowly the clothesline
started moving. One by one, Perla caught
each egg and carefully placed them in a big
straw basket.

"It's working! It's working!" she cried
happily.

And it would have worked perfectly, if Lucifer hadn't suddenly shown up to cause trouble!

A loud scream from Mert startled all the mice. "Gus! Jaq! Perla! Luke! Look out! Lucifer is here!" he cried.

Lucifer had silently crept up into the kitchen. He smiled and licked his lips. The cat looked like he was ready to pounce!

Luckily for the mice, Bruno came to the rescue. He snarled and growled at Lucifer, who leaped out of the way.

But all of the commotion interrupted everyone's concentration. The clothesline suddenly swayed back and forth – and an egg fell out of a shirt pocket!

Gus didn't waste a second. He closed his

eyes, leaped off the ledge and held out his arms. He caught the egg just before it crashed onto the floor!

"Phew! That was a close call!" Gus exclaimed, wiping his forehead.

With Bruno standing guard – and keeping Lucifer away – the mice quickly moved the rest of the eggs into the kitchen. Cinderella returned shortly, carrying a pail full of milk.

"Good work, everybody!" she told them when she saw the basket full of eggs. "I knew you could do it!" She gave them a proud smile.

Now that they had all the ingredients, Cinderella and the mice went right to work making the cakes. Soon they had bowls full of thick, golden cake batter. Then the mice helped Cinderella pour the batter into small, shiny tins. She carefully placed each tin in the hot oven.

"Keep your fingers crossed that the cakes bake quickly," Cinderella told the mice as she glanced at the clock. "We don't have much time!"

Gus looked at the clock, too. It was almost three o'clock. There were dozens of little cakes in the oven. But how would they decorate them all before the baker arrived to pick them up? He was going to be there in two hours! There was only one way to get it done: they were going to need even more help.

Then Gus spotted a bluebird sitting on the windowsill, chirping happily. He ran up to it. "Cinderelly needs more help! Go get some more friends!" he told the bird.

The bluebird chirped again and quickly flew away to deliver the message to the other birds in the garden.

While the cakes were baking, the mice helped Cinderella make frosting in all different colours. Gus and Jaq sat on the egg- beaters and pedalled them as if they were riding bicycles, while Suzy and Perla added the sugar and vanilla. Then they spooned the frosting into pastry bags to get ready to decorate the cakes.

Ding! All of a sudden the timer rang. Cinderella carefully took the cakes out of the oven. They smelled delicious!

"Now we just need to wait for them to

cool," Cinderella said as she anxiously looked at the clock again. "Then we can decorate them. If we frost the cakes while they're still hot, the icing will melt, and it all will turn into a big mess!"

Suddenly, the sound of chirping filled the room. The little bluebird was back – with more of her friends.

"The birdies will help decorate the cakes, Cinderelly," Gus explained proudly. He looked at Cinderella and smiled.

Cinderella beamed. "What a good idea, Gus! And if the birds fly around the cakes, their wings will fan them – and cool them off."

And that's exactly what happened! The bluebirds happily flew around the cakes, and soon the treats were cool enough to decorate.

"Phew! Not a moment too soon," Cinderella said. "The baker will be here in less than an hour!"

"Don't worry, Cinderella," Jaq said. "Watch this!"

Jaq climbed onto a pitcher on the table. Then he jumped off and landed on a pastry bag filled with frosting.

Splat! The icing squirted onto a cake.

Cinderella clapped her hands. "Perfect!" she exclaimed. Not only were they getting the job done, but they were all having fun doing it, too!

Soon all the cakes were decorated. But before Cinderella and the mice had a chance

to taste one, suddenly there was a loud knock at the front door.

"Oh, dear!" Cinderella cried. "I told the baker to pick up the cakes at the back door. And he's early, too! I'd better get him to the kitchen before Stepmother comes downstairs! Everybody – hide!"

The birds flew out the window, while most of the mice ran toward the high rafters near the ceiling. From there, they would be able to see and hear everything that happened in the kitchen. Only Gus and a few of his friends stayed on the counter. They all hoped the baker would like their cakes!

Chapter Seven

Cinderella hurried to the front door. But when she opened it, she got a big surprise. The baker wasn't standing on the doorstep. It was Madame Gilmore with the new rosebush. In all the excitement about baking the cakes, Cinderella had completely forgotten that Madame Gilmore had promised to deliver the rosebush that afternoon. But luckily the florist hadn't forgotten!

"Hello, Madame Gilmore!" Cinderella

exclaimed. "Lovely to see you again. And thank you very much for coming over so quickly!"

"I'm sorry I'm late, my dear," the florist replied. "There was quite a commotion in town this morning. Tonight's dessert for the fair was destroyed, but the baker has promised that there will be a delicious dessert just as good as the one he made earlier. Everyone can't wait to see what it will be!"

Cinderella smiled to herself. "Well, I suppose we'll just have to see what happens at the fair tonight," she said. "Thank you again for bringing the rosebush. Let's go out to the garden so we can plant it."

"No, no, my dear, I know you're very

busy," Madame Gilmore said. "Just point me in the right direction and I'll take care of everything."

"Of course! It's just around the corner," Cinderella replied gratefully. She pointed at the cobblestoned path that led to the garden.

As Cinderella walked back into the house, she heard another knock – this time coming from the back door. She hurried to answer it.

"Now surely that's the baker," she said as she ran back to the kitchen. "I hope Stepmother didn't hear the second knock. I don't want her to come downstairs until all of the cakes are gone – and the new rosebush is planted!"

Sure enough, the baker was standing at the kitchen door. He looked very nervous.

"Hello," he said. "Is the dessert ready?"

"Yes, it is," Cinderella replied with a smile. "Come in. I hope you're pleased with what we've done. I think that it really turned out wonderful!

The baker stepped into the large kitchen. His eyes grew wide as he took in the sight: dozens of beautifully decorated cakes that almost looked too good to eat!

"How – how did you do it?" he said with a gasp. "It's not possible . . ."

"Oh, I had a little help from some very good friends," Cinderella said. She glanced over at Gus and winked.

"May I try one?" the baker asked, pointing

to one of the cakes. "They look delicious." He licked his lips in anticipation.

"Certainly," Cinderella replied.

The baker took a bite of the tiny cake. "Mmm," he said with a grin. "Scrumptious! You must share your recipe!"

"I'd be happy to," replied Cinderella. "But right now, we need to pack up these cakes and get them to the fair!"

Cinderella and the baker carefully loaded the cakes onto silver trays. Then they carried all the trays to his wagon.

"Thank you so much," the baker said. "Will I see you at the fair tonight? I want everyone to meet the young lady who created such wonderful desserts. You have truly saved the day!"

"Well . . . maybe," Cinderella said slowly. She really wanted to go back to the fair, but she hadn't finished her chores yet, and there was still so much work to be done.

"You must come to the fair," the baker insisted. "And bring your friends, the ones who helped you make the cakes. Thank you again!" He climbed onto the seat of the wagon and set off for the village.

"Cinderella!" Madame Gilmore called from the garden. "I'm finished planting the rosebush. It looks absolutely beautiful!"

Cinderella walked over to her. The rosebush did look perfect. "Oh, Madame Gilmore, thank you!" Cinderella cried.

"You're very welcome, my dear," Madame Gilmore replied.

Cinderella waved as Madame Gilmore also set off towards the village. What a busy day it had been!

Now, the sun was just starting to set. Cinderella walked back into the kitchen. All the mice were sitting on the counter, eagerly waiting for her.

"We did it," Cinderella said happily. "Thank you for all your hard work. And Gus – thank you very much for your good ideas this afternoon. You're going to fit in perfectly around here."

Gus grinned up at Cinderella. "I wish we could go to the fair tonight, Cinderelly," he said. He looked at the other mice, who nodded sadly.

"I know, Gus," Cinderella replied. "I'd love to go to the fair, too. But I think there's just too much work to do around here. Stepmother will never let me spend the evening at the fair when I haven't finished my chores. And speaking of Stepmother, I should show her the new rosebush."

Cinderella walked out of the kitchen and

headed towards her stepmother's room. Oh, I just know that she'll love the flowers! she thought.

Chapter Eight

Cinderella nervously climbed the stairs to the second floor of the mansion. She knocked quietly on Lady Tremaine's bedroom door. "Stepmother," she said. "May I come in?"

"Yes, you may," Lady Tremaine called. "Come on in."

Cinderella stepped into the bedroom and found her stepmother lying down with a cool cloth over her forehead.

"I'm sorry to interrupt you, Stepmother," Cinderella said. "But there's something in the garden that you should see right away."

Lady Tremaine's eyes flew open. She jumped off her fancy canopy bed. "Oh, no," she said. "What is it now?"

Cinderella hid a smile as she followed Lady Tremaine out to the garden. Her stepmother gasped when she saw the beautiful new rosebush.

"Stepmother, it was an accident that all the roses were cut off the other rosebush," Cinderella told her. "I'm very sorry that it happened. I went to the village this morning and got you a new one. I hope you will accept my most sincere apology."

Lady Tremaine looked at Cinderella and gave her a small smile. "Yes, I accept your apology," she said. "Thank you for replacing my rosebush. It was the right thing to do." She paused. "Did you finish all of the chores you were asked to do today?"

"No, Stepmother," Cinderella said sadly, staring at the ground.

"Well, I suppose the chores can wait until tomorrow," Lady Tremaine replied. "You may have the evening free. But make sure you get them done in the morning."

"I will, Stepmother. Oh, I most surely will!" Cinderella cried happily. "Thank you!" She rushed back downstairs towards the kitchen and grabbed her basket. "Gus! Jaq! Everybody!" she called. "I have wonderful news!"

"Lucifer is getting a new home?" Jaq asked hopefully.

Cinderella laughed. "No, silly – better than that," she said. "Stepmother says I can have the evening free. I'm going to the fair!"

The little mice were quiet. "Oh," Gus said softly. "Have a good time, Cinderelly."

"And you're all coming with me, of course," Cinderella continued. "Come on, hop in the basket. We've got to hurry or we'll miss the big parade!"

"Hooray!" cheered the mice as they leaped into Cinderella's basket.

Cinderella hurried down the lane towards the village, carefully carrying the basket. All the mice were chattering excitedly about the fair.

"I want to see the Prince!" cried Perla.

"I want to see the big parade!" Jaq announced.

"And I want to eat some cake," Gus added. He rubbed his belly. "Yummy!"

When Cinderella and the mice reached the village, they heard the sounds of the band playing as they marched in the parade. There were crowds of people everywhere, talking and laughing as the parade slowly moved down the narrow streets of the village.

Cinderella held the basket up so that the mice could peek out and see everything. "Oh, look!" she cried. "There's the royal carriage. The Prince and his family are leading the parade!"

As the carriage passed by, Cinderella waved to the royal family along with the rest of the crowd. She turned to watch the carriage continue its journey to the village square – and saw something even more exciting. Right in the middle of the square were all the little cakes that she and the mice had made. They were beautifully arranged on a table.

"Our cakes," she whispered to the mice. "Don't they look beautiful? I hope the royal family likes them, I really do!"

As the carriage came to a stop, a hush fell over the crowd. The royal family stepped out. The men bowed and the ladies curtsied.

"Welcome, everyone," the King grandly announced. "The village fair has officially begun!"

The crowd burst into cheers and applause.

"And I see here that our village baker has outdone himself, as usual," the King said. He admired the little cakes.

"Your Majesty, I must confess that these cakes are the work of some promising young bakers in your kingdom," the baker gently corrected the King with a low bow.

"Indeed?" asked the King with a smile. "I will decide how promising these young bakers are by tasting one of these cakes." The crowd was silent as the King picked up a cake and took a bite. Cinderella held her breath – and so did the mice.

"Delicious!" the King proclaimed. "One of the best cakes I've ever eaten." He turned to the baker. "Well done for finding such talented new bakers and introducing them to the village. And now, everyone, please enjoy the fair!"

"Did everyone hear that?" Cinderella whispered into the basket. "The King loves our cakes. We did it!"

The mice were delighted. Gus looked over at his new friends and smiled. What a day!

The royal servants made their way through the crowd and passed out the little cakes. Cinderella took two from the tray – one for her, and one for the mice to share. She took a bite of the cake.

"It really is as tasty as everyone says," she whispered to the mice.

"Mmm, very tasty, Cinderelly," Gus said happily. As he spoke, he sprayed a mouthful of crumbs into the air.

"It's really good," added Perla. "Really, really, really good!"

"And you know what else?" Cinderella continued. "I think it tastes even better because we worked so hard together. I couldn't have done it without you – all of you!"

"I just have one question," Jaq said as he licked pink frosting off his paws.

"Yes, Jaq?" Cinderella replied.

"Can we get another cake to share?" he asked hopefully.

Cinderella laughed. "Oh, I don't see why not," she said. "After all, those talented new bakers deserve to have a little more cake if they want some!"

Cinderella smiled as she looked around at all the people enjoying the desserts. Even the King was reaching for a second helping! Cinderella was so relieved that everything had worked out. It had been such a busy day, filled with some mishaps and surprises – but the ending was sweeter than she ever could have imagined!

Don't miss the next enchanting Disney Princess chapter book!

Belle

The Mysterious Message

*I*t had been another lovely dinner at the Beast's castle. Although Belle did wonder if she'd ever get used to singing and dancing plates!

Belle sat at the long dining-room table. She held a cup of hot tea in her hands. The Beast had gone off to bed long ago. Most of the dishes and forks and knives and spoons had already washed up and put themselves away.